To my gifts in life . . .

My love and soulmate of all journeys, Michael, and
our creations, Ella and Leo. You make life magical and
unforgettable.

Thank you for inspiring me and encouraging me to reach
the next level. I carry your light with me wherever I go,
and I love you beyond words.

NATI

Santa Barbara, California
2022

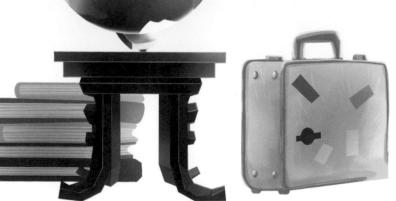

THiS
ADVENTURe
BELONGS
TO:

_____

ISBN 13: 978-1-63489-551-4

Library of Congress Catalog Number has been applied for.
Printed in China
First Printing: 2022
26   25   24   23   22   5   4   3   2   1

Creative direction: Marc Friedland
Illustrations: Guillermo Alonso
Editor: Eric La Brecque

Wise Ink Creative Publishing
807 Broadway St. NE
Suite 46
Minneapolis, MN 55413
wiseink.com

WRITTEN BY
Nati Smith

ILLUSTRATED BY
Guillermo Alonso

CREATIVE DIRECTION
Marc Friedland

EDITOR
Eric La Brecque

Mish loved to cook more than just about anything.

"When I'm in the kitchen," she said to herself, "all my worries melt away."

Mish had her own special way of creating delicious dishes.

Some people read recipes.

Mish trusted her memory.

Some people used measuring cups.

Mish followed her **heart.**

3

When she saw the sign for the big cooking contest, Mish couldn't believe her eyes.
Grand prize:

A trip around the world!

LOOKING for passionate COOKS

"I know just what to cook to impress the judges," Mish said with a smile.

"My famous shakshuka."

Cooking plus travel, what could be better?

With her heart as her guide, she advanced first one round and then another.

Next came the finals.

5

Mish remembered the Sunday mornings when she made shakshuka with Mama and Papa.

She could see Mama cracking the eggs

and Papa chopping the vegetables.

6

She could see the little bowl of spices, too, that she added to the dish.

Their fragrance tickled her nose. They were her own secret blend.

Afterward, she could smell the rich scent of the shakshuka baking in the oven.

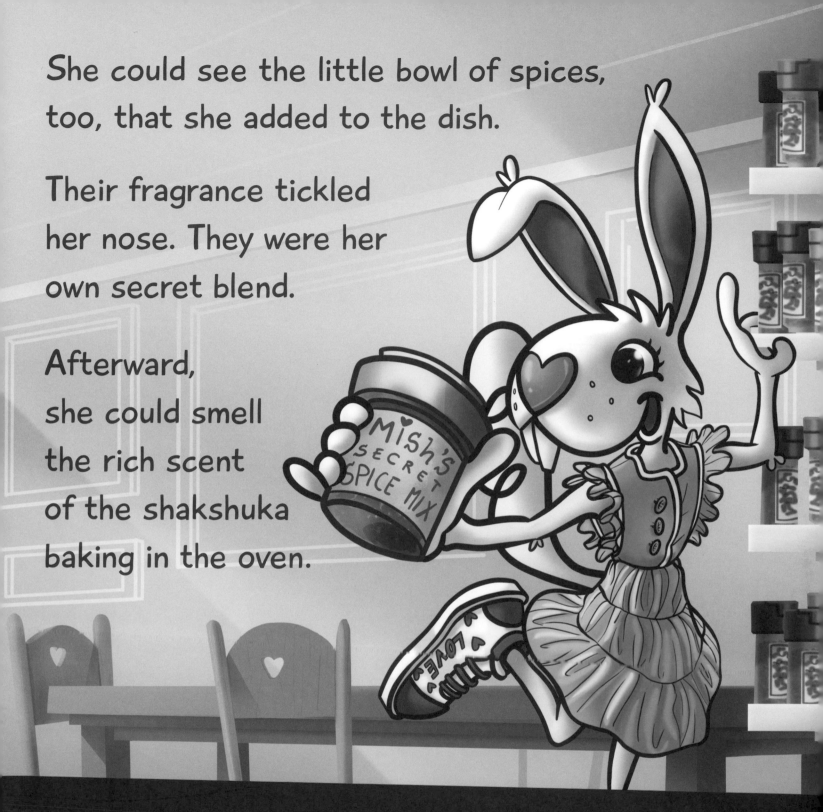

Remembering made her feel warm all over. Every person has their own special love language. Cooking was Mish's.

To prepare for the contest, Mish made shakshuka over and over again. The night before the contest, she practiced one final time.

"What's this?"

she cried in disbelief as she opened the oven door.

"How did my eggs end up so runny?"

"It's just nerves,"
Mama said,
giving her
a hug.

"I think somebody forgot
to cook from the heart,"
Papa said gently. "When you
cook from the heart, that's all
you need to succeed."

"I know I can do it," Mish thought as she lay in bed that night.

She pictured making the perfect shakshuka step by step. Then she imagined herself traveling new places and making new friends.

As she grew sleepier, one final thought stayed with her:

"I must remember my most secret ingredient,

my . . . secret . . . ingredient . . .

my . . . secret . . .

in . . . gredi . . . ennnnnt . . . Love."

She was fast asleep.

The next day, Mish arrived at the finals feeling calm and confident. The two other finalists, Gigi and Elliott, were already preparing their workstations.

"What are you making today?" Mish asked Gigi.

"Cauliflower wings," Gigi said as she set out her ingredients.

Mish's mouth watered.
"I cook only with plants," Gigi added.
"I'm vegan, you know."

14

Elliott came over to say hello. "I'm not vegan," he said, "but I believe in taking good care of the land and all the living things that depend on it."

"And what are you making?" Mish asked.

"Grass-fed filet from a cow I raised on my farm," Elliott said with a smile.

"I wish I had my own farm!" Mish and Gigi exclaimed at exactly the same time.

"Jinx!" Mish said, and they all burst into laughter.

"What about you, Mish?" Gigi asked.
"What are you going to cook?"
When Mish told her, Gigi looked confused.

"Shak—shuk—what?"
she asked.

"It's pronounced

shock-shoo-ka,"

Mish said.

"It's a baked egg and veggie dish from the Middle East."

Mish's face suddenly felt hot.

Her heart began beating faster.

If no one can even say the name of my dish, Mish thought, will they ever be able to taste the love I put into making it?

"Baked eggs and veggies!" Elliott said.

"One of my faves!"

He held out a basket filled with eggs.

18

"Take some," he offered.

"They'll add a nice bit of farm-to-table flavor to your shaka-waka-whatchamacallit!"

Mish gave Elliott a hug.

The three chefs went back to their workstations.
A gong rang out and the contest began.
Each chef had one hour
to prep, cook, and plate
their dishes.

Mish started cooking, but something felt wrong. When she looked down at her pan, she saw bits of shell in the eggs.

When she tried to remember her secret spice blend, she couldn't. Her thoughts were racing and her hands were trembling.

Mish closed her eyes and took a few deep breaths.

She remembered Elliott's warm hug and Gigi's kind smile. She remembered Mama's keen skills and Papa's wise words.

And then she remembered the missing ingredient:

Love.

"My heart is all I need to succeed!" she said.

Mish's oven timer went off just as the contest gong rang out once more. **Time's up!**

Mish looked into the oven. Yes, there they were: her eggs, baked perfectly, and the sauce all around them was happily bubbling away.

Mish held hands with Gigi and Elliott as the judges tested their dishes. They **oohed** and **ahhed** over everything they tasted.

Gigi had made a tangy hot sauce with her cauliflower wings.

"Holy smokes! Flavorful and fresh!" the judges said.

Along with his filet, Elliott had roasted multicolored carrots with herbs from his garden. "Vibrant and earthy!" the judges said.

Then they came to Mish's shakshuka. After each of them sampled it, they shared a long look and nodded.

"Gigi and Elliott, your dishes are truly inspired," the first judge said. "You have a bright future ahead of you."

"As for you, Mish," the second judge said, "your magic shakshuka has touched our hearts in a way no other dish ever has."

"Congrats and best wishes!" the third judge piped.

When the contest was over and the judges
went home, the three friends shared a hug.
"Let us know where you go and who you meet,"
Gigi said.

"Keep a journal with all the new recipes you discover," Elliott said.

"I couldn't have won without the two of you," Mish told them.

Her new friends smiled. Mish was ready for her next adventure to begin.

NATI SMITH

Born an Aquarius in Jerusalem, author Nati Smith has always been a spiritual seeker and is constantly inspired through mindfulness, well-being, and soulful expansion. She is a believer in serendipity and followed her heart to the US, where she lives with the love of her life and two magical children in the land of uni and avocados (also known as Santa Barbara).

Her love language is cooking and baking. Happiness is sharing meaningful time with her friends and family, having dance parties in the kitchen, running, traveling, tuning in to endless podcasts, making fun playlists, and watching documentaries. Nati's mind is blown by biohacking and neuroscience, because the more you know, the more you know you don't know.

Mish is inspired by her daughter's incredible taste buds and her inseparable lovey, which she calls "Mish." After joining her daughter on each family trip and every single night's sleep, Mish has become an official member of the Smith family.

I Hope you find ADVENTURE in everything you do, every DAY...

XO,

Mish